Aunt Fanny

The Third Little Pet Book

With the tale of Mop and Frisk

Aunt Fanny

The Third Little Pet Book
With the tale of Mop and Frisk

ISBN/EAN: 9783337088569

Printed in Europe, USA, Canada, Australia, Japan

Cover: Foto ©Andreas Hilbeck / pixelio.de

More available books at **www.hansebooks.com**

Mop saves Hal's life.—**P. 42.**

Third Little Pet Book.

THE THIRD

LITTLE PET BOOK,

WITH THE TALE OF

MOP AND FRISK.

BY

AUNT FANNY,

Author of "Night Caps," "Mittens," "Christmas Stories," "Wife's Stratagem," etc., etc.

———

"I LOVE GOD AND LITTLE CHILDREN."—Richter.

———

NEW YORK:
JAMES O'KANE, PUBLISHER.
1867.

THIS TALE

OF

MOP AND FRISK

I DEDICATE TO MY LITTLE FRIEND

HOWARD,

WHO LIVES ON MURRAY HILL AVENUE.

CONTENTS.

MOP AND FRISK;

or,

THE TWO DOGS.

— ◆ ● ◆ —

IN WORDS OF FIVE LETTERS AND LESS.

MOP AND FRISK.

PART I.

THE DOGS LEAVE HOME.

 N a small town by the side of a lake, there once lived two dogs named Mop and Frisk.

1*

Frisk was a pert black and tan dog, with a tail that stood bolt up in the air, and a pair of ears to match; while Mop was a poor old cur, with a head like a worn-out hair-broom; ears like bell-pulls; a mouth that went from ear to ear, and a great bush of a tail. Then he had to drag the cart of an old rag-man round the town, to earn his meals; while Frisk, who lived with a pie-man, had a fine ride in the cart each morn; and all the work he had to do was to bark at the bad boys who tried to steal the pies. The rest of his time he spent in play.

One day the old rag-man, who was as cross as ten bears,

and far too fond of beer, came
out of a shop where he had
been to drink, while poor Mop
had to wait in the cold. The
rag-man's legs went from side
to side; he could not walk;
so he got in the cart, on top
of all the rags, and cried to
Mop:

"Come, go on, you bad
cur, or I'll make you!" and

with these words, he let fall
a great stick on the back of
the poor dog, and gave him
a kick with his thick hob-nail
shoes. Mop tried to start, but
it was more than he could
drag. Down came the stick
once more; and this time,
made quite wild with pain, he
gave one yelp and one jump,
broke the old ropes that held

him to the cart by a great
jerk, and made off down the
road like a flash. The bad
old man did bawl to him to
come back; but Mop was too
wise for that, and did not stop
to see if the wind was west
or not, till he came to a part
of the town which was quite
new to him.

The place where our dog

now found him-self was a
sort of blind court, with the
blank wall of a house on each
side, and, worse than all, with
not the sign of a thing to eat
to be seen.

"A fly to snap at would be
a good thing," said the poor
dog with a sigh. "I think I
could eat a bit of brick, if I
could get one up. But cheer

up! it will all come right in time! I'm *free* at least—that is one good thing!" and he gave three jumps and three barks for joy, so loud that they most took the top of his head off.

Just then there came up, at a smart pace, Frisk the pie-man's dog. He held his head in the air as proud as you like. When he saw Mop, he tried to turn up his nose at him, but it was so flat, there was no turn up to it. Then he gave a loud sniff, and said with an air:

"Who are you? Where did *you* come from?"

"I am as good a dog as you," said Mop. "My coat is not quite so fine to be sure,

and my ears don't stick up
so much; but I'm a nice sort
of chap for all that. Shake
a paw."

"What! shake a paw with
such an old flop-ear as you?
You must be mad."

Mop did want to say, "You
are a pert, stuck-up cur," but
he was too well-bred; so he
made a bow, and put his paw

on his heart, and said: "I meant no wrong; but I took you for Frisk, the pie-man's dog."

"Well, so I am — or so I was, I mean, till last week; but, you see, the trade was too low for a dog of my style — with such ears and such a long tail. I was not made to bark out of the back of a pie-cart at all the rag-tags in town; so I have cut the pie-man, and mean to try high life in some big house. My own aunt lives with a judge; and it will be odd if some rich man does not like my looks, and take me home with him. But I must be off; it would not do to be seen with you, if I hope to rise in the world. A good time to you, my boy. He! he! you are such a beau, you can't fail to cut a dash. G-o-o-d day!"

"Stop a bit!" cried Mop, as Frisk ran off. "You don't think much of me *now* I see, but time may show me to be the best dog yet. What if we were each to try to find a new place, and meet here in a

month from now, to tell what
has past in the mean time ?
Don't you think that would
be a nice plan ?"

"Oh ! I'll do so if you
wish !" said Frisk ; " but don't
ask me to bow when we meet,
I beg; it won't *do*, you know."

"Shake a paw then," said
Mop.

Frisk, very loth, put the tip

of one claw on Mop's paw.
Then the two dogs stood back
to back, and, with a one!
two!! three!!! off they went
as if a mad bull was at their
heels.

PART II.

THE DOGS MEET ONCE MORE.

N the last day of the month, M o p a n d Frisk, true to their word, came to the place where they last said good-by.

But how each one did look to see if his mate were the same dog he last saw!

Mop's coat was rough no more — it shone like silk; his ears were cut; he wore a fine brass neck ring, with a new name on it; and his whole air was that of a dog in luck.

Poor Frisk was so thin that you could count all his ribs.

His tail stood up in the air no more. He hung his head and crept close by the wall, as if he did fear some one would beat him if he dared to run or jump.

Good Mop did not look on him with scorn when he saw him in this sad way; but ran up to him on three legs, with one paw held out for "How d'ye do," and his great fly-brush of a tail a-wag for joy.

"Why, Frisk, old dog!" he cried, "how glad I am to see you! How have you been this long time?"

"O Mop!" said Frisk in a sad tone, "will you speak to me now I am so poor? It is I who am not fit to be seen this time."

"Frisk, my good dog," said Mop in a grave tone, "*real* worth is not a thing of looks. Let me tell you that if I knew you to sie l a bone, you would lose my good-will in truth. But I do not look down on dogs if they are poor and good. Come home with me; we can talk more at our ease in my nice house,

where you will find some first-
rate bones, if you would like
them."

"O yes ! I guess I would !"
cried Frisk.

So the dogs set off on a
trot by the side of a fine lake,
on the banks of which the
town was built. They soon
came to a large house, with a
court-yard in front, tall green

rails all round, and a grea
gate by which to go in. There
was a small gate near the large
one, the latch of which Mop
could lift with his nose, for
Frisk and him-self to pass;
and then the dogs ran round
to the back of the house. On
one side of the yard Frisk
saw a fine dog-house, fit for
the king, with a roof that ran

to a peak, a porch in front, and a dove-cote on a pole on top. In-side there was a heap of clean, warm hay, and on a blue plate were some nice bones.

"There!" said Mop, "don't you call that prime? Help your-self to the bones, Frisk; I can get lots more."

Frisk did not wait to be

asked twice, but fell to, and soon made way with the legs of a fowl. When these were gone, kind Mop ran to the house and got a beef-bone for him. Poor Frisk ate as if he was not used to such fine fare, and the good dog Mop, who gave up his own meal to feed Frisk, felt as glad as if he had had it all him-self.

When Frisk had made an end of the bones, he and Mop laid down in the dog-house; and as Frisk had asked him to do so, Mop told his tale, as you shall hear.

But first he asked Frisk to rise, so he could put more of the soft hay on his side. "Do you feel quite warm?" he asked.

2*

"O yes! thank you, dear Mop," said Frisk; "as warm as a toast. You will make me cry, if you are so kind to me. When you were poor, I was a cross dog to you. Oh! I can not bear to think how bad I was;" and a great big tear came out of each of Frisk's eyes, and ran off at the end of his nose.

"Oh! that is all gone. We will be. kind old dogs now, and do all the good we can in the world. And now here goes for the grand tale of all my joys and woes since I saw you."

MOP'S TALE.

"You know, Frisk, that when we left the court, you chose to go in the town, and

I by the lake. I felt sad to think I had no one to care for me in the world. But my watch-word is, 'Don't give it up!' and I could not think that all would leave me to want a bone. So I laid down by the road-side, in hopes to see some one who would take care of me.

"First, I saw a man on a

fine horse; and as he had no
dog, I said to my-self, 'Who
knows but what he wants one
to keep the flies from his
horse's legs!' So I ran by
him a short way, when—would
you dream the man could be
so bad?—he gave me a cut
with his whip, that made me
hop and yelp for pain. 'Serve
you right for a vile cur!' he

said with a loud laugh, and on he rode.

"Next came a blind man; but he had a dog to lead him. The blind man's hat was laid on the ground, and when a cent was put in it, the dog gave one bark; when two cents were put in, he gave two barks, and so on. So, you see, there was no room

"There was no room for me, and I had to trot on."—P. 38

Third Little Pet Book.

for me there, and I had to trot on.

"At last I saw a small boy and girl trip down the road, hand in hand, with their nurse close by them. They wore such fine coats and hats, that it was plain they were rich; but when the boy put his small hand on my head, and said, 'Good dog,' and the

girl did the same, I knew they
must be kind too.

"So I ran by them, in
hopes they would speak to
me once more.

"There were some wild
rose-buds on the bank of the
lake, and when the girl saw
them she cried: 'O Hal! just
see those sweet rose-buds!
How nice they look! They

have just come out! Won't
you pick me a few?'

"'Yes, dear May,' said
the boy; and he let go her
hand and ran to where the
rose-buds grew.

"'Don't go there, dear
child,' cried nurse; 'you may
fall in the lake.'

"'No I won't! I'll take
care,' cried Hal; and as he

spoke he bent way down the bank. O me! the earth gave way, his foot did slip, and ere the nurse could run to his aid, the poor child fell, with a loud cry, in the lake.

"There was no time to be lost; and, more glad than I can say, that I was on the spot, I leapt in the lake, swam to the side of the child, and

in as short a time as it takes
to tell, I had his coat in my
teeth, and got him safe to
shore.

"The nurse took her dear
boy in her arms and cried for
joy; and May was so glad
that she put her arms round
my wet head, and gave me a
long hug.

"'We must take the good

dog home with us, Miss May,'
said nurse, 'and tell your pa-
pa what he has done for Hal.
And now let me wrap my
shawl round you, Hal, and
then we must all run home as
fast as we can, for fear you
may take cold.'

"We were soon at this
house, where Mr. and Mrs.
Grey, the pa-pa and mam-ma

of Hal and May, live; and
nurse soon told them how I
had saved the life of their
dear son.

"You may think how great
was my joy to have them call
me, 'Good dog! brave dog!
the best dog in the world!'
and give me a hug and say I
must live with them from that
time.

"So Mr. Grey sent me out with Hal to the yard; and he got Jim, the groom, to wash and trim me, while May ran to ask the cook for some meat to feed me. The dear child did wish so much to make me glad, that she tied her own white bib round my neck to keep me neat while I ate, and fed me with her own hand;

"She fed me with her own hand."—P. 16.

Third Little Pet Book.

while Hal, and a wee bit of a girl, who came to see them, did look on.

"It was not quite as much to my taste as hers to be fed; but she was so full of the fun of it, that I would not for the world have made one growl.

"Next day their pa-pa got me this nice house, and Hal put round my neck the brass

ring you see me wear; which
they say has on it: 'To Dash,
the good dog, from Hal and
May.'"

When Mop, or Dash, as we
must now call him, had come
to an end, Frisk drew a deep
sigh, and said: "Well, Dash,
as that is your name, if I had
been as good as you, I might
be as well off by this time;

but I think, when you hear
what a sad l'fe I have led for
the past month, you will say
I am well paid for my fine
airs to you. So now to my
tale."

FRISK'S TALE.

"I made haste to the best
part of the town, when I left
you and the court, and, late
in the day, found my-self in

3

a fine place. Near the best
house was a group of three
small boys; they were at
play with some small, round,
smooth stones; and when one
stone hit the next, a boy
could cry out: 'That is mine!'

"Well, for my sins, I came
to a halt just in front of these
boys.

"'Oh! oh! look at that

"Near the best house was a group of three small boys."—P. 50
Third Little Pet Book.

nice dog!' cried one whose name I found was Bob. 'I guess he is lost. I mean to have him for my dog.'

" 'No, you shall not,' said Ned, the next in size. 'He shall be my dog.'

" 'No, he shall be mine,' said Sam. 'I want him! I *will* have him!' and on that they all tore up the steps of

the house, and burst in-to a
room where their mam-ma
was, with:

"'Ma, I want the dog!'

"'Ma, give me the dog!'

"'No, no, no, ma!—me!
me! me!'

"'O dear! what a noise!'
said their mam-ma. 'Do be
still. If you want the dog,
take him; but don't whine,

or go on as if you all had the tooth-ache.'

"All this time I was such a gump, I sat quite still; but when I saw the boys come out and rush at me with rude words, I said to my-self, 'Come on, Frisk; I do not think it will do to get a new place here.' So I made up my mind to take to my heels:

when, O my dog-star! down
came a great bat on my head,
and the three boys fell on me
all at once; grab'd me by the
ears, tail, and one leg, at the
same time, and would have
torn me to bits, I am sure, if
their mam-ma had not come
and made Bob and Ned let
go.

"I was put in the front

room then, in a whole skin,
and here, in spite of all he
could do, I broke from Sam
and hid my-self at the back
of a couch that stood by the
fire-place.

"'Now what's to be done?'
said Sam.

"'Let's hunt him out with
sticks,' said Ned.

"'Good! come on!' cried

Bob and Sam; and with-out more words, Bob armed him-self with the broom, and Ned and Sam got canes, as if they were in chase of some wild beast, and all flew, with a loud whoop! to bang poor me out of my strong-hold.

"I don't know what would have been my fate, if I had not hit on what to do just in time. The sides and front of the couch, by good luck, came down past the seat, and bands of broad tape were put from side to side, to keep the white slip in its place. I gave a jump, made out to land on the tapes, and sat on them in great fear lest they might give way.

" It was well I did so ; for

3*

the boys made their sticks fly from side to side at such a rate, that the first blow would have been the death of me. This game went on for some time, till they were quite at a loss to know why I did not come out or make a cry.

"'Why where *can* he be?' cried Sam. 'Look and see, quick!'

"Ned went down on his knees—'Why he's gone!' he said with a gasp.

"'O the b-a-a-d thing!' cried Sam. 'Ma! ma! our dog's lost! Boo! hoo! hoo!' and to my great joy, all three left the room to treat their dear 'ma' to a howl. Oh! how I *did* long to snap at their legs.

"By this time so much fluff
and dust had got up my nose
in my close nook, that I was
fit to choke; and as the boys
were gone, I dared to come
out. There was a large arm-
chair close by, with a deep,
soft seat that was just to my
taste. ' I hopt in, laid down,
and was soon in a fine nap.

"Think, then, what was my

state of mind to wake up with
a yell and a land-slide on top
of me! Up flew a fat old
dame from the arm-chair,
where she had just sat down,
as if she was shot! Bang!
came a great gilt book, that
she let fall in her start, right
on the end of my poor tail, as
I leapt to the floor! 'E-e-e!'
went she; 'yi! yi! yi!' went

I; and 'Hur-ra! here's the dog!' cried Ned, as he came bang in at the door, caught me by one ear, and ran up to the top floor with me in wild joy; which put the last touch to my woes!

"Once in their play-room, the bad boys made me drag a toy-cart full of dirt, ran straws in-to my ears, beat me

with sharp sticks, and shot
peas at me out of a pop-gun.
They kept up these nice plays
till tea-time; when they were
so kind as to let me go, and
treat me to a few old scraps
of cold meat for my share of
the meal.

"When tea was done, their
mam-ma bid them go right
to work and learn their tasks;

and, with pouts and whines from all three, they sat down. As soon as their mam-ma left the room, Ned took out of his desk a mouse-trap, with a poor wee mouse in it, all in a shake of fear, and cried: 'Here, Sam, just see what I've got! An't that gay?'

" 'What? what? let me look!' cried Bob, who had

"Ned took from his desk a mouse-trap."—P. 64.

Thad Little Pet Book.

sat till now with his legs
spread out, and a book be-
fore him up-side down.

"'No, you shan't. Go
'way!' said Ned, in a whine.

"'I will! I will!' Bob did
bawl; and as he spoke he did
jump up and give Ned's hair
a great pull! Then Sam gave
Bob a punch, and the three
boys did fight and kick each

other at a fine rate; in the
midst of which pow-wow I
left the room, and ran off
down the back stair.

"Here the maids were
more kind to me than the
boys; for cook made me a
nice soft bed in a box, and
gave me some bones to pick;
while Jane, the maid, took
me in her lap, and let me

sleep there, snug and warm, till she went to bed.

"But you could no more guess what the next day had in store for me, than you could say how deep the sea is; so I will tell you.

"Just as Jane came in with the tea-tray, and cook had got a tin pan to pour me out some milk, down came

those vile boys full tilt, to
grab hold of me once more.
The kind cook asked them
to let me be, till I had had
my milk; but she might as
well have asked the wind not
to blow; and with Bob to
hold me, and Ned and Sam
to mount guard on each side,
they made haste once more
to the play-room.

"When they had me safe, and the door shut, Bob cried in great glee: 'Now, boys, I tell you what we'll do: let's play our dog was a slave, that we had caught just as he was on the point to run off. We will tie him by the fore paws and flog him well.'

"Oh! oh! how I felt when I heard these words! My

hair stood on end with fear.
I threw my-self on the floor,
and cried for help. Ah me!
no help came. One would
think they might have felt
for a poor dog that could not
help it-self. But no; they
were with-out heart.

"Bob found a cord, and
tied my feet to a large nail
in the wall. Ned and Sam

did each fetch the strap that
they had round their task-
books, and then these bad
boys beat me till I felt as if
I must die.

"At last they heard their
mam-ma call from her room,
'Boys, boys, come right to
your tasks—it is past nine
o'clock;' for she did teach
them her-self I found out.

At the sound of her voice,
they left off, and ran to the
door to beg for a short time
more.

"Now was my time at last.
I freed my paws by a great
jerk, shot past Sam's legs,
flew down the stair, and out
of the house; for by great
good luck, Jane had just gone
to the door to let in the post-

man. I am glad to say I
sent Sam too down the stair
like a shot, with a boot-jack
and a pair of tongs, which
Ned and Bob threw, and which
were meant for me, at his
heels. This made up, in part,
for the pain he had put me
to. But, oh! how sore and
lame I was! I sank on the
earth when I was clear out

4

of sight, and felt as if my death was near. If it had not been for what next took place, my end would have come that day; but as I lay there all in a shake, I heard a child's voice say: ' O dear Fred! here is such a poor dog! Just see! he looks half dead! Let us stop and pat him!'

"'Dear me! Poor toad!'
cried Fred. 'Where could he
have come from? Pat him
well; don't fear.'

"Her soft hand on my
head made me raise my eyes,
and I saw a boy and girl of
nine and ten years old. They
did not seem to be rich, but
they were just as neat and
nice as two pins, and their

kind looks and words made
me feel sure they were good.

"'Poor dog! I fear he
wants food,' went on Nell. 'I
mean to give him a bit to eat,
Fred.'

"'Let me feed him too!'
cried the boy. 'Here, take
my knife and cut some bread
for him.'

"Nell took a loaf from the

bag on her arm, and with
Fred's knife cut off a good
thick slice. She gave half
to him, and they broke it in
bits and fed me by turns.

"'You dear pet,' said Nell,
with a sigh, 'how I wish I
could take you with me! But
we are too poor; it can not
be.'

"'Oh! don't you think

mam-ma would let us have
him ?' cried Fred.

" ' No, dear,' said Nell; ' we
must not think of it. Come,
bid the dog good-by, and let
us make haste home.'

" I could but lick her hand
to thank her for the food, and
as I could rise now, I felt that
it was best to run on.

" ' Good-by, you dear dog-

"Good-by, dear doggy!"—P. 78.

Third Little Pet Book.

gy!' cried both; and they did stand and watch me till I was out of their sight. Oh! how I did wish I could go home with them!

"Just as I did turn round the end of the street, I heard an odd sound ——"

Here Frisk rose in haste and said: "But I dare not stay, dear Dash; I ought now to be at home. Some day when I can get out, I will come and tell you the rest of my sad tale, for the worst part is yet to come."

"But where must you go, Frisk?" said Dash.

"Why, to the show, where I play," said Frisk.

"You play! Can you act?" cried Dash.

"Yes! come out-side. Now, just see here!" and while Dash did stare at him, with his mouth and eyes so wide open that you would not think he could close them at all, Frisk stood on his hind legs, and went thro' a jig, with a look on his face as if he had lost his last hope; then fell down on the grass, stiff and

4*

stark, as if he had been shot; got up, made a low bow, and then went lame on three legs.

"Dear me!" cried Dash, "how smart you are! Where *did* you learn all that?"

"It would take a long time to tell," said Frisk. "If I can, I will come and see you next week, and you shall then hear all. Now, good-by."

"Here, take this nice sweet bone with you," cried Dash. "Good-by, old chap. I hope I shall see you soon;" and the good dog went back to his house, full of Frisk's tale. He tried so hard to think of a way to do him some good, that he got quite a bald spot on the top of his head, and at last laid down with his nose in his paws, to sleep on it, and dream of bones without end ; for, you know, he gave up his own to feed one worse off than him-self. Good Dash ! I hope each dear girl and boy who reads this will try to be like him, for that is the way to be loved by all,

PART III.

DASH SEES A PLAY.

THE same eve, when Mr. Grey came home, he said in a sly way: "I see there is a show of dogs, who dance and act a play, in town; but Hal and

May do not care to see them,
I know."

"O yes! yes! we want to
go!" cried both at once. "Do
take us to see them, pa-pa."

"Well, get your hats then,"
said Mr. Grey, "and we will
go."

"Let's take Dash," said
May. "He wants to see the
dog-show too!"

Her pa-pa said, with a laugh, that he did not think Dash would care to see a play; but Hal and May did beg so hard, that at last he said they might take Dash if they chose.

So the two ran up the stair in high glee to their nurse, who put on May's round straw hat and silk sack, and got

her nice black mitts to put
on her wee hands.

May said, " I want to put on
my mitts my-self, nurse;" so
nurse said she might do so,
and went on to dress Hal.

But when May went to put
the mitts on, she was in such
haste, that she tried to get the
right mitt on the left hand.
The mitt would not go on, of

course, and she cried out:
"Why, nurse, this is all
wrong; it's got no thumb
at all!"

How Hal and nurse did
laugh when they saw what
May had done! May had to
laugh too, when nurse did
show her that the mitts were
quite right, if they were put
on in the right way. They

had great fun. But their pa-
pa came to bid them make
haste; so they told nurse
good-by, and ran down the
stair, hand in hand, as gay
as two larks. Dash came to
join them in the court-yard,
and soon they were all four
on their way to the show.

But, dear me! when the
an at the door of the show

saw Dash, he said: "I can't let dogs in, sir."

Here was a blow! and May, with her sweet blue eyes quite sad, cried out: "But you will let our Dash in, Mr. Show-man, won't you? You don't know what a good dog he is; he saved Hal's life!"

Now when the show-man heard dear May say this, and

saw her sweet face and blue
eyes raised to his, he could not
help a smile, and said : " Well,
for such a dear pet, I must
say, yes. Dash may go in,
but he must lie still and make
no noise. One bark, and out
he goes!"

"Oh! he will be as still
as a deaf and dumb mouse!"
cried Hal and May both at

once. So, to the great joy
of all, Dash went in. Hal and
May took their seats with
their pa-pa on a long bench,
in a large room full of gay
folks, and Dash sat on the
floor close by them.

There was a stage at one
end of the room; a fall of
green baize hung in front of
it. In a short time a bell

went " ting-a-ling ! ting-a-ling !"
and up rose the baize. Then
Dash saw a small house, with
a grape-vine at the side and
tall trees, which he took for
real ones, but Mr. Grey said
were wood and green paint.
You could see a green field at
the back of the stage, and high
hills, while the blue sky was as
clear as it was out of doors.

Mr. Grey had a bill with the names of the dogs that were to act on it, and Dash heard him read it to Hal and May. The name of the play was:

THE DEATH OF POOR JACK,

THE RUN-A-WAY.

JACK, ... FRISK.

COL. GRAPE-SHOT, ... TRIP.

THE GUARD, . . . TRAY AND WASP.

JACK'S MAM-MA, ... FAN.

THE SEXTON, ... SNAP.

THE JUDGE, ... SHORT.

Dash, when he found Frisk was to act, scarce drew a breath for fear he should lose a bit of the play, and sat so still that not a hair moved.

First, in came two dogs on their hind-legs as the guard, in red coats and caps and blue pants. They had guns too; and they had such

an odd look with their own
tails up in the air out-side
their coat-tails, and their
head held as stiff as ram-
rods to keep their caps on,
that all the folks burst out in
a laugh.

Then the guard did peep
round all the trees, and in all
the holes they could find, on
a hunt for Jack; and when

5

they did not find him, they
shook their heads as if to
say: "No one here! that's a
fact!"

At last one of the guard
went to rap at the door of
the house. He gave such a
hard knock, that he shook his
cap down on one eye, and
had to hold his head on one
side, as if he had the tooth-

ache, so as to see at all. It
made him feel so bad, that
he went off in a pet to the
back of the stage, and left
the guard whose cap was all
right to knock for him-self.
This one was so short, that
he had to make a jump and
stand on tip-toe to do it.

Out came a dog in the
dress of an old dame, who,

Mr. Grey said, was Jack's
mam-ma. She wore a black
gown, a white cap, and plaid
shawl, and had a work-bag
on her arm, or fore-leg, and
a big pair of specs tied on
her nose. When she saw the
guard, she spread out her
paws, and gave each a look
in turn, as if to ask what
they came there for.

The short guard made signs to her, to show they were on a hunt for a man who had left the camp with-out leave. The old dame shook her head at this, and put a paw on her heart, as if to say *she* hadn't heard of such a thing; but the one-eyed guard shook *his* head too, and did point thro' the door, as much as to say

that the man was in *there*, he
was sure. Then the old dame
shook her head once more,
and spread her skirt to keep
them out of the house; but
the guard were too smart for
that. They aimed their guns
at the wall of the house, to
shoot Jack if he was in-side;
and when the old dame saw
that, she moved from the

door-way, with a high squeak, and let them pass.

In they went full tilt, and the one-eyed guard, in his haste, quite lost sight of his part, let fall his gun, and ran off on all four legs! It pains me to tell that a sad yelp was heard in-side the house, as if he had got a box on the ear for this fault; and Dash could not but think that to act was not such fine fun as you might take it to be.

Soon out came the guard, with Jack held fast by both fore-legs, and the old dame at their backs, who cried with all her might and main. The run-a-way, who was Frisk to be sure, wore a coat and cap like the guard, and made a

sad noise at his hard fate.
He put his paw on his heart,
and cast up his eyes as if to
beg them to let him off; but
they shook their heads. Then
he held out both paws to his
mam-ma, and she ran to him,
put her paws round his neck,
and did kiss him as well as
she could. The guard gave
him a pull to make him come.

Frisk did kiss his paw and wave his cap to his mam-ma, who fell down in a swoon; and then they all three did march off. And that was the end of Part One.

Just as the scene was to close, the old dame did lift up her head and fore-paws and look round. When she saw it was not time, she fell down

once more; so flat, that all
the folks burst out in a laugh.
I fear they would not have
been so gay if they knew
how the poor dog was beat
by the show-man, when the
play was done, for this small
fault.

Next came a horn-pipe by
a dog in a Scotch dress. He
did it so well, that all the

folks did clap their hands, and want him to do it once more; but it was now time for Part Two of the play; and he ran off with a low bow.

When the baize was drawn up once more, the small house was gone, and a high desk was set on one side of the stage, with a bench in front for Col. Grape-shot. And at

the desk sat the judge who
was to try Jack for his life.
The dog who was judge wore
a fine black silk gown, with
white fur down the front; he
had white bands at his neck,
and a great white wig on top
of his ears, which made him
look droll, I can tell you.

And now, O dear! the deep
roll of a drum was heard, and

in came, one by one, a sad set
in-deed !

First did march the dog
who beat the drum, and next
to him Col. Grape-shot, in a
grand blue and gold coat; a
gold-laced hat, with red and
white plumes; white pants,
with a red stripe down each
leg, and a sword by his side.

Then came the guard with

Jack, and, last of all, a dog
with a long box in a hand-
cart, which he drew. O dear!
dear! this was to put poor
Jack in when he was dead.
The dog wore a black coat
and an old red night-cap;
and tied fast to one leg was
a spade. He led the poor
mam-ma by the paw, and
once in a while tried to cheer

her up; for he would lift his leg and give her a kind pat on the back with the end of his spade. But I think this did more harm than good, for each time he did so she gave a short howl, and half fell down. But now the guard, with Jack and Col. Grape-shot, were in a row in front of the judge, who waved his paw, and made a bow, as much as to say: " Go on."

Col. Grape-shot, on this, did first point to Jack, and then pat the bench he sat on, as much as to say he had bid him stay in the camp. Then he shut his eyes, and leant his head on his right paw, to show that he went to sleep, and then he made two or three quick steps to the back of the stage, to let them know that Jack had run off while he slept. Then he shut his eyes once more, woke up with a start, flew to the guard, and, with a bark and a growl and a yap! yap! yap! let them know that Jack had cut off, and they must go and find him. Then he did point to

the guard and Jack, to tell
the judge that the run-a-way
was found; and at last he
made a low bow, and spread
out his paws, by which, I dare
say, he meant that his part
was at an end.

And now it was the turn
of the judge, and he must
say what was to be done to a
man who was so bad as to run.

out of camp in time of war.
The judge cast up his eyes,
and threw up his paws, as if
it was a sad shock to him to
hear that Jack had been so
bad. Then he did point to
the guns of the guard and to
Jack, and did nod his head
as if he would nod it off. It
was too plain! Poor Jack
must be shot!

His mam-ma, when she saw
this, ran to the judge and fell
on her knees; that is, she sat
down on her hind-legs, with
her paws held out, to beg him
to let Jack off; but he shook
his head "no." Then she did
the same to Col. Grape-shot;
but it was all of no use. Jack
put his paws round her neck,
and did kiss her good-by, at

which Hal and May cried quite
hard, and then gave him-self
up to the guard. They took
him to the back of the stage,
put a white cloth on his eyes,
and made him kneel down.
Then they stood in front of
him, side by side, put up their
guns, and, flash! bang!! off
went two shots; and poor Jack
fell dead on the stage!

"Flash! bang! off went two shots!"—P. 115.

Down popt his mam-ma once more in a swoon; while the guard took off the lid of the box, and put Jack in-side, who laid as stiff as a ram-rod. The dog who drew the hand-cart put on the lid, and went off first; then the Col. and judge, arm in arm; then the guard, who had to drag Jack's mam-ma by the arms, and

didn't seem to like it much;
and last, the dog who beat the
drum and who did bang a-way
for dear life all the time.

But just as the folks were
quite in tears for the fate of
poor Jack, in came the dog
with the hand-cart full tilt,
and in a great scare; for the
lid of the box was half off,
and you could see one of

Jack's paws stuck out of a crack on top. All at once, off flew the lid, and out came Jack in a new dress, to dance a jig, and show that he had come to life once more, and was just as good as new.

Oh! how the folks did laugh at this, and clap their hands! while Jack went on to show all his queer tricks.

First, he held up both his
legs on his right side, and
took a walk with the two on
his left side; then he leapt
thro' a ring or hoop, that was
let down from the top of the
stage, and took a turn round
in the air as he went; and, by
way of a wind up, he stood
on his head in the ring, and
let him-self be drawn up out

of sight, as the green baize
came down.

O dear! how much May
and Hal liked all this, while
Dash did not know how in
the world Frisk could do it;
and when all the boys and
girls were as full as they
could hold of the fun of the
thing, Dash had as much as
he could do to keep in a

howl of grief; for, you must know, the dog could tell by poor Frisk's face that all this was no fun to him.

And now the show was done, and it was time to go home.

As they went, May and Hal had a nice long talk. May said: "O dear Hal! how I wish we had a dog that

knew how to dance! What
fun, when Sue and Kate
Brown came, to have him
show off!"

"Dear pa-pa, do buy one
for us, won't you?" said Hal.
"O my! buy that queer dog—
what was his name?—the one
that stood on two legs, and
on the top of his head, and
was shot—that one!"

When Dash heard Hal ask
his pa-pa to buy Frisk, his
heart went pit-a-pat, and he
gave a short, glad bark,
which meant, "O yes! *do* buy
Frisk!"

"But," said pa-pa, "you
know that Frisk acts 'Jack,
the Run-a-way;' and what if
I should buy him, and he
should trot off the next day!

You know Dash could not have a red coat on, and run on his hind-legs to bring Frisk back; and what would you do then?"

Then Dash did wish with all his might that he could talk. "O dear!" he said to him-self; "I would give all my ears, and half my nose, if I could let them know that

Frisk would not run off;" and then, strange to say, his love and wish to help Frisk made him get up on his hind-legs, and put his fore-paws up in the air; and he gave such a droll whine, that May and Hal burst out in a laugh, and said, "Look, pa-pa! just look at Dash! He too begs you to buy Frisk!" and then they both went and stood one on each side of the dog, put their hands up, and made such a queer whine just like him, that it was the best fun in the world to see and hear them.

"But," said pa-pa, "if the show-man will sell him to me, do you not know it would be wrong to make the poor dog keep up his tricks?"

"Wrong! why how, pa-pa?"

"Well, my dears, it seems too sad a thing to tell you, but it is too true. The show-man has to beat his dogs, and starve them, to get them to learn the tricks that made you laugh so much. You saw how thin they were, and you heard them cry out, when they left the stage. If they

made the least slip or mis-
take, they got a hard blow
for it. In this way they find
out that they must do all their
tricks quite right, or they will
have the whip laid on their
poor thin sides and heads;
and so not a day goes by that
the dogs are not starved and
made to feel the whip.

"Oh! oh!" cried Hal and

May, " we did not know that.
We would not beat or starve
a dog, or a cat, or a worm.
What a bad show-man! We
would like to beat *him*."

"Oh! I hope not," said pa-
pa. "The show-man may not
think that dogs feel as much
as we do. But I know you
will be kind to all. I know
you would not strike Dash,

if he, by chance, broke one
of your toys or hurt you in
play."

"O no ! in-deed," they both
cried; and they ran up to the
dog, and gave him a good
hug, and a kiss on the top
of his head.

You may be sure that Dash
had not lost one word of all
this talk; and he was still

more sad when he knew how
much poor Frisk had to bear.
He made up his mind to tell
Frisk to run off, and come to
him. "I will hide him in my
house till the show-man goes,"
he said to him-self. "I saw
a great ham-bone on the shelf
to-day. I know it will fall to
my share, and, oh! won't it
be good! I will give this to

Frisk, and eat bits of bread. Yes, I will save up all the nice bones for him. Was he not a good dog?

But a whole week went by, and no Frisk. The ham-bone got quite dry; and Dash was sure poor Frisk must be ill or dead.

At last one day, when Dash had lost all hope, he heard the

pit-a-pat of four small feet in the yard. He had just gone in his house to take a short nap; but, I can tell you, he made but one jump out, for there was Frisk, on all fours, to be sure, but with his blue pants on his hind-legs, his red coat on his fore-legs, with the coat-tails, one on each side of his own tail, which

was up in the air in an arch
of joy, for here he was a real,
true run-a-way.

Dash flew to meet him.
" Why, Frisk !" he cried;
" make haste — fast — come
— get right in my house.
Don't mind if you tear those
old coat-tails with the thorn-
bush. There ! that's the thing !
— here you are, all safe !

Now tell me, how *did* you get off?"

Frisk had run so fast that he could not speak; he could just pant, and lay his head on Dash's, with a look full of love. At last he said: "O Dash! I have run off in the midst of the play — the show-man struck me so hard for what I could not help—for my cap fell off—and I did think I must die with the pain. O Dash! if you knew what I have gone thro', your heart would break, and you would say, I did right to run a-way." The big tears ran down his nose, and his sobs did seem as if they would choke him; and Dash gave such a long howl of woe,

that it makes me cry as I
write these words, and I am
quite sure you will cry as you
read them.

Then Dash got out all his
best bones to feed poor Frisk,
who ate as if he had not seen
a bone an inch long in a
month.

When he had done, Dash
said: "Now, dear Frisk, if

you feel like it, tell me all you have gone thro'."

So they sat down, and while the tears ran down Dash's nose, Frisk told the rest of his sad tale.

PART IV.

THE CONCLUSION OF FRISK'S TALE.

YOU will bear in mind, Dash, that I left off where the good child fed me with bread. Well, this made me strong, and I went on my way. Soon I heard a sound, like that of a flute or fife; it was quite near, but I could see no one. All at once, a great mob of boys and men came down the road, and made a crowd close by me. I went in the midst of them to find out what it all meant. Dear me! it was some-thing queer to be sure. There was a man with a big drum fast to his back, which

he beat with a drum-stick tied
to one of his feet. In the
front of his coat was a set
of Pan's pipes, out of which
he blew the tune the old cow
died of. In his left hand he
held a whip, while in his right
was a cord, which led three
dogs. The first one was an
old dog, with bow-legs, who
when the crowd did stop, got

up on his hind-legs, and gave
a look round at the two be-
hind, who stood right up on
their hind-legs, all in a grave,
glum way. One of these was
in the dress of a girl. She
had on a large round hat, full
of big red bows. The hat
was so big, and shook so
much, that it did seem as if
her head, hat, and all, would

drop off, if it got a hard knock.

"The dog with the bow-legs wore a blue coat, a flat hat with a broad brim, and such a high shirt col-lar, that the sharp ends all but put his eyes out. He had a pair of specs tied on his black nose with twine. The third had on a cap and coat like those of a

small boy. And all did look
as if they were on their way
to be hung.

"Then the man made a jig
tune on his pipe, and beat the
drum with his foot till he was
as red as fire in the face,
while the dogs kept time with
hop, skip, and jump, with one
eye on the whip.

"The men and boys were

full of the fun. O dear! how
they did clap their hands and
laugh! and I, great goose that
I was, stood on *my* hind-legs,
to try how it felt, and kept
near the dogs all day, and saw
them dance at least ten times.

"At last, when the sun had
set, the man came to an old
house, and let him-self in with
a key; the dogs went in too,

while I stood out-side on two legs, to try to peep thro' a small crack in the door. Soon there came—oh! such a good smell of hot beef-bones. I felt as if I would give all four of my legs for just one bone.

"I gave the door a push, and found it moved; and then, to make a long tale

short, I went in ; for I said to
my-self: 'The man may beat
me to death, but if I stay
here I shall starve to death;
so I can but try for a bone.'

"I found my-self in a low,
dark room. The walls were
black with dirt and smoke.
The dogs lay in one part of
the room, and the man sat
by the fire. On a hook was

a great pot, and from this came such a nice smell, that all the dogs, and I with them, did lick our lips the whole time.

"And now there came in the room an old dame, with a dry, brown face, for all the world like the nut-shell dolls the pie-man's boy used to make.

"'Well, John,' she said, 'have you had a good day?'

"'Yes, Gran-ny; I took a hat full of cents. See here, what a lot of them! But that dog there, he lost me a three cent piece to-day; so he goes with-out his bone.'

"The poor dog with the bow-legs gave a great howl when he heard this; but the show-man hit him on the nose with his whip, and he slunk off, while the big tears ran in a stream down his face.

"The rest stood on their hind-legs in a row, while the old dame with the nut-shell face took the pot from the fire.

"'Here,' said she to the show-man, 'hold the dish while I pour the stew out.'

"Oh! how it did smoke! and what a fine smell it had! The man got a loaf of bread and two blue plates from the shelf, and a knife and fork for each; and then they went to work to eat as fast as they could, while the dogs and I did look on with all the eyes we had. When the show-man had eat-en all he could,

he took some more meat, cut
it up in bits, and said : 'Now,
I shall give each dog a bit in
turn. Look sharp you! If
the wrong dog starts when I
call, he gets none at all. Now
then, Pete !'

"The dog in the cap made
a jump and one snap, and the
meat was gone.

" 'Now then, Hop !' said

the man; and the dog in
the girl's hat got it; and
then it was Pete's turn, while
poor Bob with the bow-legs,
who lost the three cents, kept
up a kind of soft howl and
a sob, as if his heart would
break.

"All this time I did think
I must die for want of food,
and I made up my mind to

stand on my hind-legs till the show-man gave me some meat too. So I got up and did not fall, while you could count ten, then I ran up to the show-man, and stood on my hind-legs at his side.

"'Why bless me, dame!' he cried, 'where did this dog come from?'

"'Where to be sure,' said

the dame; 'you let him in your-self.'

" ' Did I, Gran-ny? Well, that is queer. I did not see him. He seems to know how to stand up—sit down, sir.'

" Down I went like a flash.

" ' Get up, sir,' and up I got once more as stiff as a po-ker.

" ' Why don't you take him

for one of your set,' said the old dame. 'He must be lost for just see here! his name is on the brass ring round his neck.' Then she put on a pair of old horn specs to spell my name out. 'F-r-i-s-k Frisk; what a nice name! and what a clean, trim chap he is! Why, John, he would be a great help to you, he seems so smart.'

"'So he would,' said the man. 'He would soon learn to dance, and he knows now how to stand up. I can soon teach him more. Here, you, sir! take that!' and he threw me a large bit of meat, which I was glad to get, you may be sure. Then I took the rest of my share in my turn with Pete and Hop, and, O dear!

how nice it was, and how glad I was to get it!

"When we had eat all up, the show-man took off the hats and coats of his dogs, and sent them and me to sleep in a large flat box, that stood at the end of the room. It was full of straw and quite nice.

"Then the man sat down by the fire to smoke his pipe

and have a chat with his old brown nut-shell Gran-ny.

"I was so glad to rest, that I went fast to sleep right off. But, O dear! O dear! the next morn, it was sad as it could be, for I had to learn to dance a jig, and stand on my head, and he beat me so, that I had a fit. I did think he would break each bone I had, and the more I cried the more he beat me.

"But I had to learn; and in two weeks' time I went out with the rest.

"One day the same man I ran from to-day saw me dance in the street. He was a big show-man, and had dog plays, and was quite rich and great; so he tried to buy me.

I heard him tell *my* man, that the dog who used to play 'Jack, the Run-a-way,' was just dead, and I would make a first-rate Jack in his place.

"So he paid, I don't know how much, and got me, and set me to learn my part. O my dear Dash! my life was one scene of hard blows and l ard fare. The poor wee dog who acts the old dame in the play is worse off than I, for she is so weak, that she can not do her part well; and oh! how he beats her! She has told me more than once that she would be glad to die, and I get quite wild when I think I can not help her. If the bad man would whip me for her, I would be glad to take it, tho' I get blows all the time for my own share."

"Oh! how sad!" cried Dash, the big tears in his eyes. "What a bad, bad man! How glad I . am you have run a-way from him. But what shall we do to hide you?"

"Dear Dash, if you will keep me here for four or five days, I may get some one to

take me, who is as good and
kind as Mr. Grey, and then
some day I will try to show
you how much I feel what
you *have* done and *will do*
for me."

"Don't speak of it," said
Dash. "It is as much of a
joy to *do* good as to have
good done to one's self. You
shall stay here with me, dear

Frisk! and we will wait and see what comes of it."

"O you good old dog! you dear Dash! I will stay in your house all the time. I will be as still as a drum with a hole in it."

"Yes, and I know you will come out all right at last. I tell you what! I heard May and Hal ask their pa-pa to buy you. O my! they want you so much!"

"Do they? O dear! then I can stay here all the rest of my life." And in his joy he tried to stand on his head; but the roof of the dog-house was too low, and his legs came down on top of Dash's back, and gave him quite a start.

"But," said Dash, "I must

tell you that May and Hal
said you were to dance for
them."

" O dear! if that is all, I
will dance the whole day for
a good home."

So the two dogs kept house
for a week, and Dash went
out and got the bones, while
Frisk made the straw beds,
and swept the scraps out with

his paws for a broom. Not the tip' of his nose did he show in the day-time, but at night he took a run round the lawn to get the twist out of his legs.

The fat old cook in the house said she did not know how Dash could eat so much; for he would beg for bones five or six times a day. She was

a good old soul, and she gave
him all the bones she had, and
he would lick her hand and
wag his tail, and all but speak
to thank her.

At last one day, Dash heard
Mr. Grey say that the show-
man had gone a-way. He
had tried his best to find
Frisk. He said he would give
a large sum to get him back;

and all the boys in town went out ·to hunt the poor dog. But they did not find him, as you and I know.

PART V.

AND now, as I shall tell you, one day May and Hal went out on the lawn, when lo! there stood Frisk, first on his hind-legs, and then on his head; then he danced

a jig, and then ran up to lick
their hands.

"O my! O look! here is
that dear Jack we saw in the
play," cried May.

"Yes, so it is! Why, Jack,
where *did* you hide all this
time?" said Hal, and he gave
him a soft pat, and May put
her white arms round his
neck.

Tears of joy stood in Frisk's eyes, and he ran with May and Hal and Dash up to the house, where their pa-pa and mam-ma were.

You may be sure the two went hard to work to kiss and coax pa-pa to let Jack or Frisk stay. They asked him to look how thin the poor dog was, and how sad it would

be to send him back to the
show-man, who would beat
him, and may-be kill him, he
would be in such a rage.

"O now, dear pa-pa! do
let him live with us!" they
cried; "*we* will not beat him,
and he may dance or not, as
he likes. Come, we will kiss
you ten times;" and they both
got his face down, and gave

them to him on each cheek at
the same time, and made him
and mam-ma laugh so, they
could not speak a word for
quite a while.

Well, the end of all this
long tale is, that Mr. Grey
wrote to the show-man, and
said he had got his dog, Frisk,
and he would like to keep
him. I do not dare to tell

you how much he said he
would give to buy him ; but
it was such a large sum, that
the show-man took it. And
now Jack—Frisk, as they call
him — and Dash have each
a house to live in, but they
eat and take their naps in one,
for they love to get as close,
side by side, as they can.
Frisk stands on his hind-legs

and his head, and does his jig
dance in great style for May
and Hal, and all the boys
and girls who come to see
them. If *you* want to see
him, you must speak quick;
for I fear he will soon be so fat,
with all the nice bones and
kind words he gets, that his
hind-legs won't hold him up.
But of this you may be quite

sure, that Frisk and Dash will
have a good home as long as
they live, and when they die
of old age, if you don't cry
for their sad loss, May and
Hal will; for, you know, Dash
saved Hal's life; and life is
dear to the young when they
have no sad times, but joy
and fun each day.

And now May, and Hal,

and Dash, and Frisk, must bid
you good-by. If you want
to hear how they get on, you
must come and tell me, and
if you give me a good kiss,
I will let you know.

Good-by! my dear pets!
May the good God bless you
all.

www.ingramcontent.com/pod-product-compliance
Lightning Source LLC
Chambersburg PA
CBHW031105020726
47495CB00007B/2051